CEPHALOX
THE CYBER SQUID

BY ADAM BLADE

ORCHARD

With special thanks to Brandon Robshaw

www.seaquestbooks.co.uk

ORCHARD BOOKS
338 Euston Road, London NW1 3BH
Orchard Books Australia
Level 17/207 Kent St, Sydney, NSW 2000

A Paperback Original
First published in Great Britain in 2013

Sea Quest is a registered trademark of Beast Quest Limited
Series created by Beast Quest Limited, London

A CIP catalogue record for this book is available from
the British Library.

ISBN 978 1 40831 848 5

1 3 5 7 9 10 8 6 4 2

Printed in Great Britain by CPI Group (UK) Ltd, Croydon, CR0 4YY

The paper and board used in this paperback are natural recyclable
products made from wood grown in sustainable forests. The
manufacturing processes conform to the environmental regulations of
the country of origin.

Orchard Books is a division of Hachette Children's Books,
an Hachette UK company

www.hachette.co.uk

TEN YEARS EARLIER . . .

>LEAPING DOLPHIN, DIVELOG ENTRY 176.43

LOG BY: Niobe North
MISSION: Find the legendary city
             of Sumara
LOCATION: 1,603 fathoms deep.
             Co-ordinates unknown.

We don't have much time. This may be
the last entry I make. We're stuck
on the ocean bed and both engines
have failed.

The *Leaping Dolphin* is surrounded by
ocean crawlers. Hundreds of them.
They're attacking. They're scraping
at the hull. It's only a matter of
time before they break through.
Unless Dedrick can get the engines
started again, it's the end.

If this tape is ever found – if it
ever reaches you, Callum, and Max –
I want you to know I love you, and

>LOG ENTRY ENDS

CHAPTER ONE

BENEATH THE WAVES

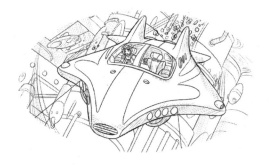

Rivet's iron head rose from the waves, water streaming off his snout. His electronic bark echoed around the walls of the mighty city of Aquora.

"Hey, Rivet, what's up? What's the matter?"

Max leant over the rails, and Rivet stared back up at him, still barking, eyes flashing red. The dawn light gleamed on the water. Max loved coming down to sea level in the early morning with Rivet to fish, before his dad was awake, and the city was up and buzzing. Rivet was a brilliant fisherdog. Max had programmed him to be. But no fish had ever got him this excited.

"What's up, boy?" said Max. "What have you seen?"

"Don't know, Max!" Rivet barked.

Max had equipped his dogbot with a few simple phrases. Rivet must have seen something he didn't have a word for. He turned and swam a little way off, propellers churning madly. Then he came back, gazing up at Max. He barked again, and his stumpy metal tail wagged.

"You want me to follow you?" Max asked.

"Yes. Follow."

There was a docking bay close to where Max stood – a pair of giant steel 'fingers' that held a small submersible craft, bobbing about in the water. It belonged to the AMRS – Aquora Marine Rescue Service. Max recognised it as the latest model, a ZX200 Sea Lion. It was a beautiful piece of engineering, strong enough to resist the crushing water pressure at the very bottom of the ocean. Max had always wondered about the mysterious world below the waves, but had never had the chance to see it for himself – subs were strictly out of bounds to him. But what harm could it do to borrow it? As long as he wasn't caught.

Max looked around. There was nobody about, so he vaulted over the rail and landed on the gunmetal-grey deck of the sub. He admired its streamlined stingray shape as he felt around the edge of the plexiglass dome. He found the right button and pressed it. The dome opened smoothly and silently and Max slid into the leather driver's seat.

Out in the water, Rivet barked excitedly.

"Hang on, Riv – just let me start this up."

A Marine Rescue Officer would use an electronic card to activate the craft. Max didn't have one, but that wasn't going to stop him.

He switched on the sub's computer and the screen glowed green. It wanted a password. No surprise there. Max found the control panel for the password system. His fingers flew over the keyboard as he set it to *Accept Engineer Password*.

Please insert engineer's password, the computer said.

Max keyed in the engineer code. His dad was Head Defence Engineer in Aquora, which meant he had access to a lot of codes – codes that Max had seen and memorised.

Max gave a broad grin as the engine roared into life.

"Easy when you know how," he murmured.

The plexiglass dome closed over his head, and with a jolt the metal fingers parted, releasing the craft.

Max had never piloted a sub before, but the controls were simple and well designed, and he knew he could handle it. Still, he felt his heartbeat quicken as he headed out into the open sea.

Rivet dived beneath the waves, the water closing over the top of his propellers. Max took a deep breath and shoved the throttle forwards. The submersible dipped, accelerated and shot down into the water. The force of the engines threw Max back in his seat.

The deeper he went, the darker it got. He flicked on the Sea Lion's searchlights, and a powerful beam cut through the water, showing Rivet swimming ahead. Max felt a thrill of excitement. He'd never been underwater before. Dad would freak out if he knew! His father hated the ocean; he didn't even like Max to go swimming in it. Ever since Max's mother and uncle had taken a sub on a secret mission ten years ago – a mission from which they'd never returned.

Max had been two years old when that happened. He hardly remembered his mum, yet deep inside he still missed her. She was a warm, loving presence who had disappeared from his life without warning.

She and her brother had gone to search for the legendary underwater city of Sumara, home of the Merryn – a mythical race of sea people. At least, most people believed they were mythical, because no one had ever seen them.

Yet down here in the dark water, with fish drifting across the yellow beam of the searchlight, Max could almost believe in the Merryn. The ocean was so vast and deep. *Who says they're not real?* he thought. *Who can say for sure what lives down here?*

He shivered. If the stories about the Merryn were true, he didn't want to meet them. It was said that they had strange and dangerous powers. They hated humans and wanted to harm and enslave them. Max remembered his old nanny saying to him, "If you don't behave, the Merryn will come and get you!"

Rivet dived deeper and deeper, swimming quickly. What had he found? Sometimes he drifted out of the path of the searchlight, but he sent back regular pulses of electronic sound which beeped across the sub's sonar screen, telling Max exactly where he was.

"Good boy," he murmured, though Rivet couldn't hear him. "Good dogbot!"

Rivet was keeping close to the walls of the city, which extended all the way down to the ocean bed. They passed apartment windows. The poorest people lived here, far below the surface of the water. It was weird to see people living underwater, as if they were in a

goldfish bowl. He passed a window and saw a man and woman in their kitchen. They looked thin and undernourished, and wore workers' overalls. Max accelerated, hoping they hadn't seen him. If they spotted a twelve-year-old boy piloting a submersible, it would be their duty to report it to the authorities.

Lights glimmered along the giant building – gantries for maintenance workers, steel doors, underwater docking bays, mechanical millwheels for extracting the wave energy on which the city was powered.

It's amazing that we built all this! Max thought.

His people had learned to survive in a world that wasn't their natural home. And not just survive – the elite of the city enjoyed lives of luxury above the surface, where Max and his dad had an apartment. They lived on Level 523, one of the highest spires of the city – thanks to his father's important post as Aquora's Head Defence Engineer. Max thought of the underfed couple he'd just seen in the kitchen, and felt a squirm of discomfort. He and his dad were so lucky compared to them.

His thoughts were interrupted by another of Rivet's sonar barks beeping across the screen. Max steered towards it. He saw Rivet in the searchlight, but there was something else there, too, in the darkness beyond.

It looked like... Could it be a person? Yes – a girl with long hair waving in the current. Rivet had found a dead body...

But no. The girl was *moving*. She was swimming along the city wall, peering in through the portholes. Impossible! How could anyone get this far down without diving equipment? How could she breathe?

The girl turned towards the sub's searchlight, gave a flip of her feet and, quicker than Max would have thought possible, she was suddenly right up against the plexiglass dome, staring in at him.

She had smooth skin, large eyes, white,

even teeth, and her long silver hair billowed
around her face. She wore a costume made
of some plaited green material and... Max
gasped. There were gill-like openings on each
side of her neck. Her hands, which pressed

against the plexiglass dome, were webbed.

A Merryn, Max said to himself in disbelief. *I'm looking at a mythical Merryn!*

CHAPTER TWO

ATTACK ON AQUORA

The Merryn girl opened her mouth. Max scrambled to switch on the sub's external microphone. A singsong blend of sighs and whistles filled the cabin. It sounded like a recording of whale song Max had once heard, but softer. It was beautiful, but he couldn't understand a word she was saying.

He shrugged helplessly.

Anger crossed the girl's face. She repeated her singsong speech louder, more urgently.

"I don't understand," Max mouthed. "I don't speak your language." If it *was* a language.

The girl turned and pointed away from Aquora.

Max found the control that rotated the searchlight. The beam swept through the black water, lighting up shoals of silvery fish and…what was that in the distance?

It was a vague, dark shape, like a cloud of ink. It was writhing and changing form, getting bigger all the time. It was coming towards the sub! A little closer and Max would be able to see it clearly.

"ALERT! ALERT!" The sub's radio crackled into life, making Max jump. "ALL AQUORA SERVICE PERSONNEL REPORT TO LEVEL ZERO IMMEDIATELY."

Max groaned. Someone must have noticed the missing submersible. He'd be arrested as soon as he docked and his dad would go ballistic when he found out what Max had done.

There was a slim chance that if he got to Level Zero before the port cops, he could dock and make himself scarce. He'd have to head back right away, and investigate the mystery of the Merryn girl later.

"I'll be back – see you here!" he said to the girl. She wouldn't understand that, of course. He pointed downwards with both forefingers, trying to get across the idea of 'here'. She gazed at him blankly. *Does she have any idea what I'm trying to say?* he wondered.

There wasn't time to find out. Max turned the sub, whistling into the microphone to call his dogbot. Rivet came alongside, propellers whirling.

Max took one last glance behind him at the strange shape. It seemed to have too many legs. Could it be a group of creatures, not just one? A knot of sea snakes? Something about it made him shudder. For a moment he felt a twinge of guilt for leaving the Merryn girl alone, but he couldn't stay.

He pushed the throttle lever, and the Sea Lion accelerated, leaving the girl behind. *I'll find her again later*, Max promised himself. He cut the motor and nosed the submersible

into the docking bay. The steel fingers gently closed around it. He threw open the glass dome and jumped onto the dock, with Rivet scrambling up after him.

There was no chance of getting away undetected. The walkways were heaving with people. Sure enough, a man was striding towards him, dressed in the blue uniform and peaked cap of the Aquora City Cops.

"What are you doing here? Don't you know we have a Red Alert situation? All civilians are to evacuate Level Zero!" he said.

"Oh," Max said. He wasn't in trouble after all. Something else was going on, something more important than a borrowed submersible.

He ran to the central concourse where the high-speed lifts were, with Rivet scampering at his side.

Crowds were rushing towards the lifts, pushing and jostling, talking nervously.

They looked scared.

"What is happening?" yapped Rivet.

"What's going on?" Max asked a woman as she ran past him.

She barely slowed as she answered over her shoulder. "There's something big on the scanners approaching the city! We have to get inside."

"The defences aren't ready!" said a man in a frightened voice.

A squad of Aquora City Defence Officers in black uniforms came marching across the concourse. Max's dad had once told him that the Special Issue Blasters they carried were powerful enough to knock a hole in the side of a building. Unlike everyone else, they were going towards the waterfront, not away from it.

"There's no need to panic!" a Defence Officer shouted out. "Engineer Callum is on his way down to activate the defensive shield."

Engineer Callum was Max's father. He felt a surge of pride that the city's safety depended on his dad.

"What's attacking us, exactly?" he asked the Defence Officer.

"That's classified. Just get out of the area. Quickly now!"

The officers marched off in the direction of the waterfront. Max joined the throng of people queuing for the lifts, wishing he could stay and find out more about what was going on.

Max saw his father striding through the crowd. The people of Aquora parted respectfully before him. Half a head taller than anyone else, he looked impressive in his smart black uniform with golden braid.

"Dad!" Max ran to his father, catching him up by the waterfront. "What's going on?"

"Max! Where have you been?" he said. "Go

back to the apartment right now."

"Not till you tell me what's going on!" Max replied, folding his arms.

Max's father sighed, and drew Max away from the crowd. "Don't spread this," he said. "I don't want to start a panic. We think the city is about to be attacked by some kind of... monster."

Max felt his heart rate quicken. "Maybe

I can help—" he started to say.

"No, Max. There's nothing you can do. Will you just get out of here before it's too late?"

Crash! Something exploded out of the ocean. A mighty wave broke over the waterfront, drenching Max and his dad, and a huge, black tentacle reared up from the waves. It was thicker than a man's body and longer than any watersnake Max had ever seen.

He ducked as the tentacle swept along the docking area, knocking cops and Defence Officers flat. One man tumbled into the ocean with a cry.

The ocean seemed to boil. More enormous, swaying tentacles burst out of it. The Defence Officers opened fire with their blasters, but the shots bounced harmlessly off the creature's skin, which must have been tougher than body armour to resist such firepower.

Max saw that the ends of the tentacles were fitted with attachments. One had a grabbing metal claw. Another ended in a sharp, glittering spike. Others had energy cannons which fired sizzling heat-beams at the Officers. There was a ragged scream as one man was vaporised on the spot.

"Get down!" shouted Max's dad. He pulled Max behind the steel fingers of a docking bay. One of the tentacles towered above them. It had a camera on the end, which swivelled this way and that, searching.

"What on Nemos is going on?" Max asked. "What's it looking for?"

"I have to get the emergency shield up. It might hold that thing for a while. Stay there!" Max's dad sprinted across the waterfront towards the Control Centre.

The camera eye swivelled in his direction. It flashed green. *As if it's spotted what it was looking for*, Max thought. *As if—*

"No!" Max cried – too late.

The tentacle with the grabbing claw swooped down and gripped Max's dad around his waist.

He was lifted up into the sky, legs kicking helplessly.

CHAPTER THREE

UNDERWATER PURSUIT

Max leapt out from behind the docking bay. Rivet raced alongside him.

A cop shouted "Get down!" but Max ignored him. He wasn't going to hide and watch his dad being carried off by a sea monster.

Another black tentacle slammed down on the dock in front of them, making the decking shudder. At its tip was a blaster cannon pointed in Max's direction. He threw himself towards it, grabbed the blaster attachment and twisted. The beam sizzled harmlessly up into the sky but the tentacle rose and Max felt his feet leave the ground.

Rivet darted underneath, raced along the dock and leaped up at the tentacle that held Max's dad. The dogbot fastened his metal jaws onto the monster's black flesh.

"That's it, Rivet!" Max called down. "We've got to save Dad!"

The tentacle Max was clinging onto smashed down towards the ground. He jumped clear at the last moment, rolling out of reach.

As he scrambled to his feet he saw that the tentacles were slithering back over the edge of the dock and into the sea. Max's dad was held just above the water. Rivet hung on, swinging from side to side.

The monster was going to head back into

the open sea, and soon it would be gone. *It's fast, but not as fast as a submersible,* Max thought.

The sub he'd borrowed before was still berthed where he'd left it. He jumped in.

"No!" someone shouted. Two cops ran

towards him at full pelt.

Max punched in the engineer code as fast as he could, and pushed the throttle lever. The engine roared into life, and Max shot off after the monster. *You're not taking my dad from me*, he thought. *I won't lose him as well as Mum.*

The monster sank lower in the water, then submerged, taking Rivet and his dad with it.

A jolt of horror hit Max in the gut. How long could his father last underwater? A minute, at most.

But if the monster wanted to kill his dad, why hadn't it already crushed him with its claw?

Max dived, and everything got darker as his craft descended. He pushed the throttle lever to maximum. He overtook a shark that twisted in the water to snap at him. The sub's searchlight picked out the writhing black mass ahead of him.

Of course, he realised, *this is the strange shape I saw when I went underwater the first time!* The Merryn girl must have been trying to warn him. That was strange. The legends Max had been taught said that the Merryn hated all humans – but the girl had tried to warn him of the attack.

They were far out to sea now. Max imagined how his dad must be feeling, lungs bursting, unable to breathe. He had to do something, and fast.

His fingers found the torpedo launch button. He lined up the monster in the cross-hairs on the launch system's screen. A direct hit might kill the monster, or hurt it enough to make it let go of his dad.

He fired.

Two torpedoes streaked through the water. There was a twin explosion of yellow and

orange flames, spreading like underwater clouds.

Max pumped his fist in the air. "Got you!" he shouted out.

The creature stopped. Was it dead?

No – in fact, it had turned round and was swimming towards him. Max got closer and closer, still hurtling along at full speed. He couldn't see his dad. Perhaps he'd broken free and swum up to the surface...

The monster was huge, even bigger than he'd thought. A giant squid-like creature with eyes the size of portholes. Its mantle – the tall, cone-shaped body above its head and tentacles – had a kind of harness over it. The harness was made of silver metal, and the straps plugged directly into its black body. *Some sort of cyborg*, Max thought. *Half animal, half machine. Which means someone must be controlling it. But who?*

Just then, he spotted a glass bubble on top of the harness, and inside it – Max gasped with relief – were his dad and Rivet.

So the squid, or whoever was controlling it, wanted his dad alive. It hadn't been a random attack on the city. His dad had been kidnapped!

Max's dad was gesturing at him, telling him to turn back. *Easier said than done*, Max thought as he hit reverse – but still the creature drew closer.

Something crashed with brutal force against the side of the submersible.

Max was thrown from his seat. The beam of the submersible's searchlight swayed through the dark water, picking out the shape of a coiling black tentacle. *That must be what just hit me*, Max realised. The submersible was still tumbling over and over from the impact. Max rolled around inside, desperately trying to grab the throttle and regain control.

His head crashed into the plexiglass dome.

Everything went darker still…

There was a trickling sound. Freezing cold water swirled round Max's legs. He opened his eyes and fumbled for the control panel. He pushed buttons and the thrust lever, but nothing happened.

No sound, no light.

The engine was dead and the hull was cracked.

His heart was thumping. He'd have to open the dome and swim for it. He had no idea how deep he was. *But it's my only chance!* he thought.

He took a deep breath and pulled at the catch. The dome didn't move.

He tugged harder.

It was stuck fast. Black water seeped into the cockpit.

CHAPTER FOUR

THE MERRYN TOUCH

The water was up to Max's knees and still rising. Soon it would reach his waist. Then his chest. Then his face.

I'm going to die down here, he thought.

He hammered on the dome with all his strength, but the plexiglass held firm.

Then he saw something pale looming through the dark water outside the submersible. A long, silvery spike. It must be the squid-creature, with one of its weird robotic attachments. Any second now it would smash the glass and finish him off...

There was a crash. The sub rocked. The silver spike thrust through the broken plexiglass. More water surged in. Then the spike withdrew and the water poured in faster. Max forced his way against the torrent to the opening. If he could just squeeze through the gap...

The jet of water pushed him back. He took one last deep breath, and then the water was over his head.

He clamped his mouth shut, struggling forwards, feeling the pressure on his lungs build.

Something gripped his arms, but it wasn't the squid's tentacle – it was a pair of hands, pulling him through the hole. The broken plexiglass scraped his sides and then he was through.

The monster was nowhere to be seen. In the dim underwater light, he made out the face of his rescuer. It was the Merryn girl, and next to her was a large silver swordfish.

She smiled at him.

Max couldn't smile back. He'd been saved from a metal coffin, only to swap it for a watery one. The pressure of the ocean squeezed him on every side. His lungs felt as though they were bursting.

He thrashed his limbs, rising upwards. He looked to where he thought the surface was, but saw nothing, only endless water. His cheeks puffed with the effort of holding in air. He let some of it out slowly, but it only made him want to breathe in more.

He knew he had no chance. He was too deep; he'd never make it to the surface in time. Soon he'd no longer be able to hold his breath. The water would swirl into his lungs and he'd die here, at the bottom of the sea. *Just like my mother*, he thought.

The Merryn girl rose up beside him, reached out and put her hands on his neck. Warmth seemed to flow from her fingers. Then the warmth turned to pain. What was happening? It got worse and worse, until Max felt as if his throat was being ripped open. Was she trying to kill him?

He struggled in panic, trying to push her off. His mouth opened and water rushed in.

That was it. He was going to die.

Then he realised something – the water was cool and sweet. He sucked it down into his lungs. Nothing had ever tasted so good.

He was breathing underwater!

He put his hands to his neck and found two soft, gill-like openings where the Merryn girl had touched him. His eyes widened in astonishment.

The girl smiled.

Other strange things were happening. Max found he could see more clearly. The water seemed lighter and thinner. He made out the shapes of underwater plants, rock formations and shoals of fish in the distance, which had been invisible before. And he didn't feel as if the ocean was crushing him any more.

Is this what it's like to be a Merryn? he wondered.

"I'm Lia," said the girl. "And this is Spike." She patted the swordfish on the back and it nuzzled against her.

"Hi, I'm Max." He clapped his hand to his mouth in shock. He was speaking the same strange language of sighs and whistles he'd heard the girl use when he first met her – but now it made sense, as if he was born to speak it.

"What have you done to me?" he said.

"Saved your life," said Lia. "You're welcome, by the way."

"Oh – don't think I'm not grateful – I am. But – you've turned me into a Merryn?"

The girl laughed. "Not exactly, but I've given you some Merryn powers. You can breathe underwater, speak our language, and your senses are much stronger. Come on – we need to get away from here. The Cyber Squid may come back."

In one graceful movement she slipped onto Spike's back. Max clambered on behind her.

"Hold tight," Lia said. "Spike – let's go!"

Max put his arms around the Merryn's waist. He was jerked backwards as the swordfish shot off through the water, but he managed to hold on.

They raced above underwater forests of gently waving fronds, and hills and valleys of rock. Max saw giant crabs scuttling over the seabed. Undersea creatures loomed up – jellyfish, an octopus, a school of dolphins – but Spike nimbly swerved round them.

"Where are we going?" Max asked.

"You'll see," Lia said over her shoulder.

"I need to find my dad," Max said. The crazy things that had happened in the last few moments had driven his father from his mind. Now it all came flooding back. Was his dad gone for good? "We have to do something! That monster's got my dad – and my dogbot too!"

"It's not the Cyber Squid who wants your father. It's the Professor who's *controlling* the Cyber Squid. I tried to warn you back at the city – but you wouldn't listen."

"I didn't understand you then!"

"You Breathers don't try to understand – that's your whole problem!"

"I'm trying now. What is that monster? And who is the Professor?"

"I'll explain everything when we arrive."

"Arrive where?"

The seabed suddenly fell away. A steep valley sloped down, leading way, way deeper than the ocean ridge Aquora was built on. The swordfish dived. The water grew darker.

Far below, Max saw a faint yellow glimmer. As he watched it grew bigger and brighter, until it became a vast undersea city of golden-glinting rock rushing up towards them. There were towers, spires, domes, bridges, courtyards, squares, gardens. A city as big as Aquora, and far more beautiful, at the bottom of the sea.

Max gasped in amazement. The water was
dark, but the city emitted a glow of its own
– a warm phosphorescent light that spilled
from the many windows. The rock sparkled.

Orange, pink and scarlet corals and seashells decorated the walls in intricate patterns.

"This is – amazing!" he said.

Lia turned round and smiled at him. "It's my home," she said. "Sumara!"

CHAPTER FIVE

THE SECRET CITY

So this was the fabled city his mother had set out to find, years before. *She was right all along*, Max thought. *If only she could have lived to see this.* A painful lump grew in his throat.

They descended further into the city. There were thousands of Merryn. Max gazed in fascination. Some swam purposefully, carrying large clam-shells under their arms. Max saw a Merryn man guiding a shoal of puffer-fish along, just like farmers led flocks of sheep on the cultivated areas of Aquora. There were shops selling trays of different-coloured seaweeds. They passed a playground where Merryn children chased each other through a maze of coral. They stopped and stared as he and Lia rode past.

The buildings had arched doorways at every level, from the seabed to the highest tower. Of course Aquora was built on many levels too, but there you had to wait for lifts or toil up stairs to get to where you wanted. Here, the Merryn just swam up or down as they pleased.

It's like flying underwater, Max thought.

Lia placed her hands on Spike's neck and guided him down to a wide, spacious square in the heart of the city. There were grand buildings on every side, and in the centre a tall statue of one of the strangest creatures Max had ever seen. It stood on two flippers, with a body like a giant dolphin and a long, swan-like neck. Its head was small and ended in a sharp beak.

"This is where we get off," said Lia.

Max slid off the swordfish's back, noticing that the Merryn people milling about the square were staring at him. Some stood close together and muttered. Max knew they were talking about him, and he could tell from their expressions that it wasn't polite chat.

"They don't seem to like me much," he said to Lia.

"Ignore them."

Lia gave Spike a handful of seaweed she'd pulled from a pocket. She patted him on the head. "Go and play, Spike."

Spike flicked his fins and shot away. Soon he was gambolling with a group of swordfish on the far side of the square.

"This way," Lia said.

She led Max across the square to an avenue lined with plant fronds, waving lazily in the current.

"That was Thallos Square back there,"

Lia said. "The oldest part of the city. This is Treaty Avenue – it was built after the peace treaty with the humans."

"What treaty?"

Lia looked at him oddly. "Don't they teach you any history in your schools?"

"Yes, about Aquora."

"Ah, but that's only half the story!" Lia said. They passed under a huge arch of smooth white rock. "This is the Arch of Peace," Lia said. "It was built after the last great battle with the humans. The seas were red with blood. After that battle both sides agreed to stop fighting."

"Why isn't that in our history books, then?" Max demanded. The talk of war between the Merryn and the humans made him uneasy.

Lia gave a wry smile. "Perhaps they don't want you to know?"

Max frowned. Could it be true? Could

there really be a whole history of his people that he didn't know about?

"How long ago was this?" he asked.

"Thousands of years. After the war, it was agreed that the Merryn should keep the underwater realm, and the humans should stay above the sea."

"So I'm the first human to come here since the war? No wonder your people are staring at me!"

"Not quite the first," Lia said. "There was the Professor."

"And will you tell me who he is now?"

"He is the enemy of the Merryn," Lia said. "He found his way here once – but since then, we use all our skill to conceal our city. Here, at the bottom of the sea, our powers are at their strongest. We are masters of the ocean, thanks to our Aqua Powers. The Professor will never find Sumara without a Merryn guide – and you can be sure no

Merryn would guide him!"

That's all very well, Max thought, *but if that squid really is controlled by the Professor, I need to find him, so I can rescue my dad.* He was about to ask Lia how he could do that when she said: "Here we are."

The avenue rose up in a slope which led to a palace. It looked as if it had grown out of the ocean floor – a huge structure of towers and spires carved out of one enormous piece of coral.

"What is this?" Max asked.

"The Royal Palace," Lia said in a tone of surprise, as if he ought to have known that.

Two guards stood at the palace door. They bowed when they saw Lia and lowered their spears to let her and Max pass.

They went into a chamber, hung with pictures of Merryn kings and queens riding dolphins.

"Come and meet my father," Lia said. "King Salinus. He'll look after you. Just remember to call him 'Your Majesty.'"

Max's heart leapt. Lia's father was the King of Sumara! Surely he would be able to help Max track down the Professor and find his father. And Rivet. Max hadn't forgotten Rivet.

Lia brushed aside a curtain of dangling seaweed, and Max followed her into a lofty hall.

King Salinus sat on a throne carved from white bone, on a raised platform at the end of the hall. Guards with spears stood in line along the walls. Two of them, taller than the rest, stood on either side of the throne. A number of Merryn in rich robes – courtiers, Max guessed – sat near the King on smaller seats. They were talking, but a hush descended as Max and Lia entered.

In the centre of the hall was a stone plinth. It looked as if a statue or monument should have been standing on it. But it was empty.

The King looked older than Max had

imagined Lia's father would be. His eyes were stern and unforgiving and he wore a crown of pearls. As Max drew nearer, the King sat upright, the colour draining from his face.

"Father, it's all right—" Lia began.

"Guards!" The King clapped his hands.

The two tall guards shot forwards. Within seconds, the tips of their spears were pressed hard against Max's throat.

CHAPTER SIX

THE SKULL OF THALLOS

"Father! What are you doing?"

"You have given this Breather the Merryn Touch!" the King said angrily. "Don't you know what could come of that? Turning him half-Merryn? Have you forgotten the Professor?"

"I had to do it, to save his life!" Lia argued.

"The life of a Breather is worthless," the King said. This drew a murmur of agreement from the courtiers. "Not only that, you have been foolish enough to bring him here – to Sumara – to the palace itself!"

"Your Majesty—" Max began.

"Silence, Breather!" the King commanded. The spears at Max's neck pressed a little harder.

"Just because the Professor is evil, doesn't mean all humans are evil," Lia said.

"Enough," King Salinus said. "Guards! Take the Breather to the prison cells. And – and the Princess. Lock them both up."

There was a buzz of noise from the courtiers.

"Father, how can—"

"You have endangered the safety of the Merryn. You must be punished, as any Merryn would be punished."

Max noticed that he didn't look at his daughter as he spoke.

"Your Majesty, don't blame Lia—" Max

began. The guards seized his arms and dragged him out of the hall, with Lia alongside.

They were taken through another seaweed curtain at the side of the hall and down a long, dark corridor. The corridor went steeply downhill, growing colder and colder. Soon Max guessed they were beneath the seabed. The guards swam with them through a maze of tunnels. The rocky walls were covered in algae which gave off a dim green glow.

Finally, they arrived at a small prison cell, cut into the rock. The guards pushed them inside, and locked the barred door with a key of carved stone. Max and Lia were left alone in the cell, which had nothing in it but a couple of boulders to sit on. The water was freezing. Max shivered. Lia drifted over to a boulder and sat down with her head in her hands, looking miserable.

"I – I'm sorry," Max said.

"What for? It's not your fault, it's my stupid dad."

Max thought of his own dad, kidnapped and locked away somewhere – perhaps in a cell just like this one – by the Professor.

"So come on," he said, "Tell me more about the Professor. Your father said he was given the Merryn Touch – is he human, then?"

"Yes. He is an evil, clever man, who makes many strange and powerful machines."

"You mean – he's a scientist?"

Lia shook her head. "Scientists should study nature to understand it. The Professor does not wish to understand nature, but to conquer it. Like the giant squid he has turned into a cyborg. And it is us he wishes to conquer next. He has captured many Merryn and forces them to toil like slaves for him – we have heard from the few who have escaped. Somewhere in the ocean, they are building weapons which will be used to destroy Sumara!"

It's not only Merryn he's captured, Max thought. He began to understand why the Professor had taken his father. Callum was Head Defence Engineer of Aquora, an expert in weapons systems, missile launchers, force fields... *He'd be very useful indeed to the*

Professor. Max felt a surge of anger at his dad's skills being put to such evil use.

"But I thought you said Sumara was safe?" he said. "You told me the Professor would never find it, because of your Aqua Powers."

Lia sighed. "Well...not exactly. We do still have our Aqua Powers, but they are not as strong as they were. Our strength comes from the Skull of Thallos – and the Professor stole it with one of his devices. Without the Skull, our Aqua Powers are much weaker than they were. Look at my father – he looks like an old man, but before the skull was stolen he was strong and full of energy."

"So, this is an actual skull with special powers? And who in all the ocean was Thallos?"

Lia pulled a pendant out from her tunic. "Look." She showed Max a chain on which hung a golden figure. Max realized it was the same as the statue in Thallos Square – the long-necked, finned creature with the sharp beak. "This is Thallos – the Father of the Ocean. Legends say he created all of the waters and everything in them, long, long ago. Only his skull remains – but that skull has great power over all the ocean. We kept it in the palace, in the King's Great Hall."

"That empty block with nothing on it!"

Lia nodded. "That is where the Professor stole it from. When he failed to harness its power, he split the skull into four pieces, so it would be almost impossible to get back. Now, each piece is guarded by a mighty sea creature that he controls. One of them is Cephalox – the giant squid that took your father. I was tracking it when I met you."

Max was about to ask more questions when electronic barking echoed in the corridor outside the cell.

He jumped to his feet.

"Rivet!" he shouted. "Rivet!"

The dogbot came paddling into view, propellers turning, tail wagging. "Max!" he barked. "Found Max!"

"Good dogbot!" Max reached through the bars of the cell and stroked Rivet's iron ears. *I'm so glad I installed that locator chip!* he thought. "Look, Lia – this is Rivet, my dogbot! He must have escaped from the Professor—"

Lia was frowning as she stood up. "Escaped?" she said. "Don't you think the Professor would have your dogbot chained up? If your dog's got away, it's because the Professor let him go. And why would he do that?"

"I don't know," Max said.

Lia groaned. "Isn't it obvious? Because he must have guessed I'd bring you to Sumara, and he's used the dog to track us! Our Aqua Powers only conceal the city from the minds of living creatures – not robots. Thanks to Rivet, the Professor knows where we are."

There was a huge crash and the cell shook. In the distance, Max heard more crashes, and screams.

He felt a cold weight in the pit of his stomach. Sumara was under attack – and it was his dogbot that had led the Professor to the city!

CHAPTER SEVEN

CEPHALOX STRIKES

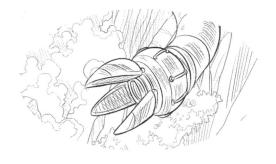

One thing's for sure, Max thought. *I'm not going to hide down here till the danger's passed.* Lia had saved his life and got thrown into jail as a reward. The least he could do was try to save her home.

First they had to get out of the cell.

"Rivet! Here, boy!"

Rivet moved closer, tail wagging, poking his metal snout through the bars. "Yes, Max! Here, Max!"

"Hold still – this won't hurt."

Max began to unscrew the control panel in Rivet's neck.

"What are you doing?" Lia asked.

"Watch!"

Max picked apart the multi-coloured clump of wires beneath the control panel. He pulled a yellow wire free and sliced through it with the penknife he always carried. Rivet's tail stopped wagging.

"No wag," he said.

"That's OK," Max said. "Just for now, I'm diverting all the power that goes to your tail to your jaws, all right?"

He made a tiny nick in a red wire, then tied the yellow wire around it so that the conductor within each wire was in contact. He screwed the lid of the control panel back on.

"Rivet – bite through these bars!" he ordered.

"Yes, Max! Yum!" The dogbot's steel jaws

clamped onto one of the bars. There was a grinding sound as Rivet ripped the bar clean away. He did the same with the bar next to it, leaving a gap big enough to squeeze through.

"That's fine, Rivet," Max told him. "You can stop now. Good boy!"

Rivet barked, obviously pleased with himself. With a section of iron bar still gripped in his jaws he looked like a dog with a bone.

"That's pretty impressive," Lia said. "But if Spike had been here I bet he could have sawn through those bars, too."

The crashing and screaming continued.

"Come on!" Max said. "We've got to do something!"

Lia led them through the maze of tunnels. There were no guards around – they must have gone to defend against the attack, Max guessed. The floor gradually sloped upwards until they emerged into the empty palace.

Lia opened a side door and swam through. Max and Rivet followed.

They were above a side street, with crowds of terrified Merryn swimming past.

"What's happening?" asked Lia.

"It's Cephalox!" someone said. "He's smashing up the city! Swim for your lives!"

Cephalox. Max's heart leapt. If the giant squid still had his dad, Max might have a chance to rescue him.

"I'm going to destroy the monster," he said. "Will you help me?"

Max barked. "Yes, Max! Fight!"

"Fight Cephalox?" Lia said. "No. It's too dangerous."

"I'll face it alone, then," Max said. "If you're too scared."

Lia's eyes narrowed. "Merryn are braver than humans! If you're fighting, I'll fight too."

They swam up the street, against the tide

of fleeing Merryn. Around the corner they came out at the front of the palace, and swam through the Arch of Peace. Max saw the huge black shape of Cephalox in the distance, at the end of Treaty Avenue. His heartbeat quickened. The squid looked like a giant spider, its tentacles covering the whole of Thallos Square. The tip of its mantle was as high as the tallest buildings.

As they swam closer Max saw that King Salinus and his guards were swimming around Cephalox, trying to stab it with spears. But their weapons bounced off the creature's tough black skin. Cephalox swiped at the guards with its clawed tentacles, scattering them. Its energy cannons blasted, vaporising sections of buildings. Masonry came free, falling in slow motion and bouncing around the statue of Thallos.

Max looked for the glass bubble on the

squid's mantle, where his dad had been held. But it was no longer there. Cephalox must have already delivered his father to the Professor.

Max's heart sank. There was no time to dwell

on it – the Robobeast had to be defeated. A direct attack would never work. Cephalox was too well armoured and had too many tentacles. Its weakness lay in the harness that was plugged into its mantle. Yes – that had to be how the Professor was controlling it. Unplug that somehow, and it would no longer be a raging monster. Or at least, that was what Max hoped.

But how could he get close?

The creature squirted out a jet of inky fluid, engulfing King Salinus and his guards in a black cloud.

"Enough!" the King shouted. "Retreat!"

The guards swam away as the ink cloud cleared. Cephalox had the square all to itself. It would spot Max straight away if he swam straight up to it.

"Spike!" Lia cried. Her swordfish swam over to her and rubbed its head against her. Rivet sniffed at Spike curiously.

Suddenly, Max had an idea.

"Lia, can you and Spike distract Cephalox while I try something?"

"What are you going to do?"

"No time to explain," Max said. "Just help me out."

"Don't give me orders!" Lia said. "I am a princess, don't forget."

Max didn't stay to argue. "Come on, Rivet!" he said as he headed towards a tall building on one side of the square. Its upper windows were level with the squid's head.

Heart pounding, Max swam around the square, keeping low so the squid wouldn't see him. He glanced back and saw with relief that Lia and Spike were swimming towards the gigantic squid.

He and Rivet reached the building and swam inside. *Cephalox won't see me in here,* Max thought. A grand staircase went up and up. He swam higher, Rivet by his side. As he rose through the building, he glimpsed Cephalox through open windows, its huge bulk blocking out everything else.

Finally, Max reached the top level. He approached the windowsill with Rivet. The top of the squid's mantle was right in front of him – the head far below, about halfway down the building. He saw that Lia and Spike were attacking the squid's eyes. *That's it*, Max thought. *Go for its weakest point*.

Close up, Cephalox looked impossibly big. Attacking it seemed a hopeless task. But if Lia could do it, so could he. He took a deep breath, said "Come on, Rivet!" and launched himself from the window, kicking off against the sill.

Before he reached the creature's harness, one of its tentacles lashed out at Lia and Spike. It caught them a glancing blow and sent them tumbling downwards.

A second later the terrifying force of the current it had created sent Max and Rivet flying. Another tentacle smashed against the wall of the building, dislodging huge blocks.

Max had to twist and turn to avoid being hit by the falling chunks of stone. He gasped in horror as one of them hit Rivet and bore him down to the ocean floor.

"Rivet!" Max shouted. He swam down after him. The dogbot was pinned down by the stone and whimpering in distress.

Lia and Spike swooped to help. Together, they managed to lever the stone off Rivet, but his leg was flattened and twisted.

"Ouch, Max!" Rivet said.

"Don't worry, boy," Max said. "We'll patch you up." He patted the dogbot's metal head.

"Look out!" shouted Lia.

Lia and Spike darted away and Max pulled Rivet to safety as one of Cephalox's tentacles

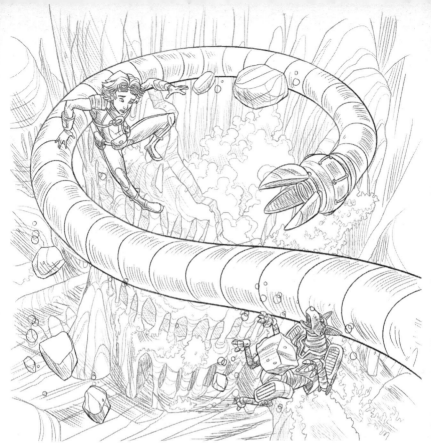

came thumping down again. The ocean bed
shook and clouds of silt rose upwards.

"We'll never get close to it with all those
tentacles!" Max said. "Unless..."

"Unless what?" Lia asked.

"Unless we can trap them," Max said.
"Come on. I think I've got a plan."

CHAPTER EIGHT

CYBER SQUID

Another tentacle came whipping down. Max, Lia, Rivet and Spike scattered. A heat beam from one of Cephalox's blaster cannons sizzled into the stonework, just missing Lia's head.

"What's the plan?" shouted Lia.

"Head for the palace!" Max replied.

Lia looked confused. "Why? That will draw Cephalox there."

"Exactly," Max said, pointing to the Arch of Peace. Understanding dawned in Lia's eyes.

"Come on, Spike!"

She and the swordfish rose through the water, avoiding the squid's waving tentacles, until they reached its huge eyes. Its tentacles lashed towards them. Lia turned and swam towards the Arch of Peace, closely followed by Spike.

Cephalox blasted a jet of water and shot after them. The jet-propelled burst of speed almost brought it up to Lia, but she and Spike stayed just ahead, swimming for all they were worth.

It was time for Max to play his part. "Let's go, Rivet!" he called.

Max swam after the giant squid, with Rivet beside him. The dogbot bravely ignored the pain signals which must have been coming from its injured leg.

Lia and Spike passed under the Arch of Peace and the squid shot after them with another jet-propelled burst.

There was a clunking, grinding noise.

"Yes!" shouted Max, clenching his fist.

The squid was stuck fast under the arch. The top of its mantle poked through, but the wider part and the ten tentacles were just too big to fit. Cephalox wriggled wildly, but could not break free. It made a violent hissing sound.

Max swam up and landed on all fours on the creature's mantle. It felt like wet, slippery rubber under his fingers. He reached for the harness and grabbed one of the struts.

Tentacles scythed up, trying to knock Max off. He ducked.

There was an ominous crunching sound. The squid's struggles were putting a huge strain on the rocky arch. Cracks appeared. Flakes of stone tumbled down to the ocean floor. Not much time... If Max didn't get the harness off soon, Cephalox would break free.

And then there'd be no stopping it.

A camera mounted on the harness swivelled and stared at Max, like an unblinking eye.

I bet the Professor is watching me, Max thought. The idea sent a surge of anger through his body, and he raised his foot and kicked. The lens shattered.

In the centre of the harness was a control panel – just like the one in Rivet's neck, but much larger. Max scrabbled at it, trying to get the metal cover off, as Cephalox bucked and squirmed beneath him. It wouldn't budge.

"Hey Rivet – can you help me out?"

"Yes, Max."

The dogbot's iron jaws crunched into the metal panel. Almost at once, it buckled and came off. Rivet shook his head, worrying the twisted piece of metal.

"Good boy!"

Underneath the cover was an array of dials, buttons and touchpads. Max stabbed at them with his fingers. Nothing happened. A small screen said *Enter Password*.

That's all I need, Max thought.

The cracks in the arch were widening. The squid's struggles became more frantic, as it sensed freedom.

Max saw a flash of white, just above the control panel. It looked like...a bone. Part of the Skull of Thallos! Max grabbed it, but it wouldn't come free. It was held in place by metal bands.

"Rivet," he said. "Can you—"

There was an almighty crack, as the Arch of Peace broke clean in two. Max watched helplessly as the two halves collapsed and fell towards the seabed in twin cascades of rubble.

Cephalox blasted a stream of water behind it and shot upwards.

Max yelled out, clinging onto the bone as he was dragged through the water.

Cephalox's tentacles swarmed around him like a nest of furious snakes. Max dodged, letting go of the bone, as one swept towards him.

Immediately another came whipping his way. He darted clear. But he couldn't go on dodging the vicious tentacles forever – they were too fast, and too many.

Wait – what if I don't dodge?

Max positioned himself right above the control panel as the next blow came. This time, it was the steel-spiked tentacle. His stomach tingled with dread as the evil, glittering weapon whooshed towards him. He waited and waited – and then, at the last millisecond, he threw himself to one side.

The spike smashed down into Cephalox's control panel.

There was a bang and a flash of light. Max was blinded for a few moments. When he recovered his vision he saw that the harness had broken in pieces and its struts had detached from the squid's flesh.

Cephalox gave itself a shake, as if it was waking from a dream. As the last pieces of the harness fell away, a glow seemed to throb off the squid's hide and it spiralled up in the water, brushing past Max and Lia. For a moment, it floated in the water face-to-face with Max. He could see what looked like a light of pleasure in the sea creature's eyes. Then it jetted up and away from the city, a graceful, streamlined creature, returned to its natural existence. Cephalox was no longer a Robobeast.

Max looked down at the wreckage of the harness and spotted the white bone, twisting and turning as it sank. He kicked his legs and swam after it, catching it easily. It was a jawbone with sharp, serrated teeth set into it.

He spotted the shapes of Lia and Spike in the distance and swam over. "Look! I did it!"

Lia put her hands on her hips. "*We* did it, you mean."

"Oh yeah," Max said. "Sorry, Lia. We did it."

Together, with Spike and Rivet, they swam to Thallos Square. Merryn were cautiously creeping back, emerging from hiding places in the ruined buildings.

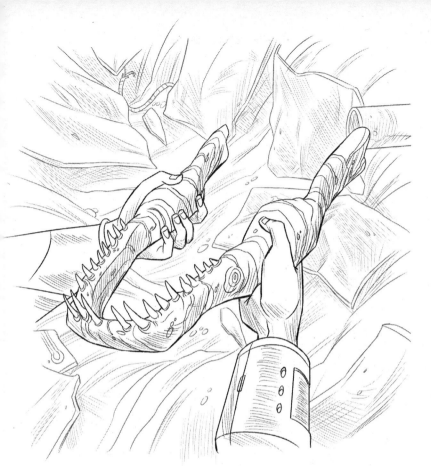

"People of Sumara!" Lia shouted. "We have regained part of the Skull of Thallos!"

Max held the jawbone up.

There was a collective gasp, then a mighty cheer. All around, Max saw smiling, relieved faces. He smiled himself. *We did it! Together.*

CHAPTER NINE

THE LEAPING DOLPHIN

At last the cheering died down. The crowd parted. King Salinus, flanked by his two personal guards, came into the square. He approached Max, his face expressionless. Max found he was holding his breath.

"You are a Breather, boy," said the King. "Of the race who are our ancestral enemies, who tried to conquer us. Your people promised to leave us to our ocean realm and keep to the surface. You are of the same race as the

Professor, who broke that promise and who plots our destruction."

"That's true, Your Majesty, but—" Max began.

The King held up his hand. "Let me finish. Blinded by these facts, I misjudged you. My daughter was right. Not all Breathers are like the Professor. You, a human boy, have saved Sumara – and retrieved one piece of the precious Skull of Thallos! I owe you an apology, and all the Merryn should thank you."

Lia ran forward and hugged her father. The Merryn were smiling and cheering all over again.

Max's heart lightened with relief. He bowed and presented the jawbone to the King, who accepted it gravely.

"And now I have something I must ask," King Salinus said. "Without the Skull of Thallos, our Aqua Powers are waning. But

you have a power of your own: the power of technology. With it, you were able to escape from prison, and to defeat the mighty Cephalox. Would you possess the courage and daring to aid us in our struggle with the Professor?"

Max didn't hesitate. "What can I do to help?" he asked.

"The remaining three pieces of the Skull of Thallos are still in the keeping of the Professor, guarded by the mighty creatures he has enslaved. With your understanding of technology, you might be able to defeat those creatures, recover the parts of the Skull, and so restore to the Merryn our Aqua Powers. We would be forever in your debt. It might go some way to repairing the rift between our people and yours. Will you accept the quest?"

Max was astonished. Was King Salinus really asking him, a boy, to save Sumara single-handed? It was true that he had defeated one of the Professor's Robobeasts – with Lia's help, of course. But could he do that again, three times? He didn't know what to say to the King.

"Wait, Father!" Lia called out. "We cannot send him on such a dangerous quest alone. He'll need a guide. Let me go with him!"

The King frowned, but then his brow smoothed. "It is fitting for children of royal blood to prove themselves willing to face peril. What do you say, Max?"

Max's burning desire was to find his father. If that meant going up against the Professor, he was prepared to do so. If it meant he helped the Merryn too, so much the better. He knew this challenge would be dangerous. But he would feel a lot safer with Lia to guide him. "Yes – I accept the quest. And I would be glad to have Lia at my side."

The crowd cheered, even louder than before.

Lia's father turned to her. "Our champion must be equipped. Will you take him to the Graveyard?"

"The graveyard?" said Max.

With a flick of her finlike feet, Lia rose high above the square. She beckoned to Max to follow. He swam up to her, but no sooner had he reached her then she was off again, glancing back once to check that he was following.

"Not so fast!" he called. "I can't keep up!"

"Do you call this fast?" Lia said. "I was going especially slowly for you!"

They swam on, Max going as fast as he was able, Lia slowing now and again to let him catch up. Soon they had left the city behind. A deep canyon appeared in the ocean bed.

Lia dived into it, and Max followed. It was dark inside, almost pitch black. Even with his improved Merryn eyesight, Max found it hard to see much. Lia's limbs were a pale glimmer in the water ahead of him. He tried not to imagine the strange creatures that might live down here in the blackness, waiting to lunge at him.

Lia came to rest on the ocean bed. Max noticed that she was making a clicking noise with her tongue. Suddenly a host of white lights appeared from cracks in the canyon walls. They were jellyfish, glowing with an eerie light.

"Wow!" said Max.

The ghostly light revealed vast heaps of equipment, piled against the canyon walls. Some of it looked antique, some new and practically unused. There were submersibles, diving suits, weapons... Max spotted the hull of a Barracuda submarine yacht, and a Mk III Frogsuit with a twenty-four-hour breathing tank. Back on Aquora he'd have done anything to get his hands on a Frogsuit like that! It was strange to think that with his Merryn powers, he no longer needed one.

"Where does all this stuff come from?"

"From Breather explorers who've tried to find Sumara – and died in the attempt. We gather it and bring it here, to the Graveyard. It's no use to us. But perhaps you could use some of it?"

"Oh, yeah!" Max foraged around eagerly. "No way!" He picked up a curved, gleaming piece of metal, turning it in his hand. It was so fine that seen end-on it almost disappeared. "A hyperblade – only the military are allowed these on Aquora. It's practically unbreakable – pure vernium. It'll cut through anything!"

He rummaged around a bit more and dug out a Lightning aquabike. It was sleek, green and streamlined – clearly built for speed. On this, he'd be able to keep up with Lia, no trouble! He sat astride it.

"What do you think?"

"What's it for?"

"It's for going through the water, really fast!"

"I can do that already," Lia said. "I don't need a machine to help me."

Max found a pair of infrared goggles and tried them on. "They help you see in the dark," he told Lia.

"Why not just call the jellyfish?"

"You can use these even when there aren't any jellyfish," Max explained.

Lia rolled her eyes. "You Breathers – you're obsessed with machines! I'd rather just use my Aqua Powers any day."

"Fine if you have them," Max said. He felt a lot more confident about the quest now that he was properly equipped.

There was one last thing he needed – something to repair Rivet's leg. He scrabbled around in a pile of scrap metal, and pounced on a chunky metal rod. "Perfect. I can replace the damaged part with this."

Then he noticed something under the rod.

A square of silver metal with ragged edges, and a picture painted on it. He picked it up.

Max felt a prickling of excitement deep inside. The picture was of a dolphin leaping from the waves. It looked strangely familiar, like something he'd seen long, long ago. His mother's sub – that had been called the *Leaping Dolphin*! And now that he thought hard, he had a dreamlike memory of being held in his father's arms, saying goodbye to his mother as she left on her voyage. The sun glinted on the plaque on the hull of her submarine. A plaque that showed a leaping dolphin…

Max realised he was holding his breath. Maybe his mother did make it to Sumara, after all? Maybe, if she'd made it this far, she could even be – he hardly dared think it – still alive somewhere?

"Have you seen this?" he asked Lia.

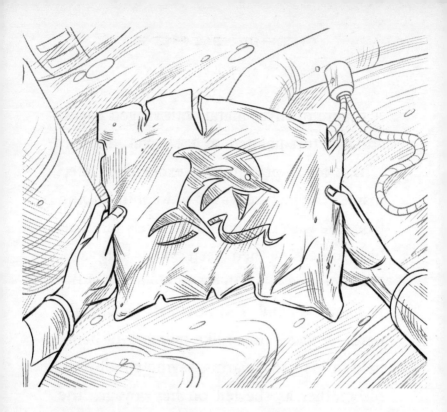

"Where's it from?"

Lia peered at the metal plaque and shook her head. "Sorry, Max. I've never seen it before. It could have come from anywhere in the ocean."

Max swallowed his disappointment and curled his fingers around the plaque. As soon as he found his dad, he would show it to him. Then he'd know for sure.

"We should get going," he said to Lia. "I'll fix Rivet up and we can leave straight away. The sooner we start, the sooner I'll find my dad!"

CHAPTER TEN

THE QUEST BEGINS

"How's it feel, Rivet?"

They had returned to the palace so Max could fix his dogbot's leg. Rivet rotated his new leg experimentally. "Good," he barked.

"Then we're ready!" Max said.

"Come, Spike." The swordfish swam up to Lia and rubbed against her hip.

"Spike's coming with us too?" Max asked.

"Of course – if Rivet can come, why not Spike?"

"Fine," Max said. "No problem."

King Salinus appeared in the palace doorway. "The people are waiting to wish you goodbye."

He led them from the palace, down Treaty Avenue, past the ruins of the Arch of Peace. People lined the street, cheering and waving. When they reached Thallos Square, Max was taken aback by the size of the crowd. It looked as if all of Sumara had turned out to wish them well. A huge roar greeted their appearance.

Max grinned and waved, hoping he looked worthy of their trust.

"You are embarking on a dangerous quest," King Salinus said. "We salute your bravery. Remember, without the Skull of Thallos, the Merryn have no control over the seas. The waters may be unruly and treacherous, and so are the creatures that live in them. You must be on your guard at all times. Not all will be as it seems."

"We'll be careful," Max said. "But how will we find the other Skull pieces? They could be anywhere in the whole ocean!"

"The Skull itself will guide you," said the King. He took out the jawbone from the folds of his robe and released it. It floated in front of him, and then slowly turned, pointing to the far end of the Square.

"Thanks," Max said. He opened the storage compartment in Rivet's back and put the jawbone inside, next to the plaque with the leaping dolphin. "Ready, Rivet?"

Rivet barked excitedly. "Ready!"

Max climbed onto his new Lightning aquabike and checked his hyperblade and infrared goggles were safely stowed in the back. He twisted the throttle and the engine roared into life.

"Goodbye, Lia," said the King. "And good luck." He hugged his daughter. "Look after each other."

"We will!" Lia said. She sat astride Spike and patted his head. "Let's go!"

Spike plunged forward. Max soon caught up on the aquabike. Together they sped in the direction the jawbone had pointed, with Rivet motoring along beside them. As they left the square, Max cast a glance over his shoulder. The King stood next to the statue of Thallos, his face smiling but his eyes sad. Tiers of Merryn floated all around the square, watching and waving.

I hope I don't let them down, Max thought.

Soon, the city was just a distant glimmer of lights in the darkness behind them. Max felt nervous, but also excited. He had no idea of what dangers lay ahead, but he felt ready to face them. He would reclaim the Skull of

Thallos and destroy the Professor's power.
He would rescue his father. And perhaps –
who knew – he would solve the mystery of
his mother's disappearance.

He looked across at Lia and smiled. She
smiled back at him.

Together, they headed out into the vast, mysterious ocean, ready to face whatever was waiting for them.

I've been waiting all my life for an adventure, Max thought, as the aquabike sliced through the water. *And now I've found it.*

SILDA
THE ELECTRIC EEL

Read on for an exclusive extract...

He couldn't let the fish get away now! Who knew where Rivet was? It didn't matter. He was definitely gaining.

The fish was heading straight for a shimmering patch of water. Max leant forward in the saddle, reaching out a hand to grab its tail. Behind he heard Lia shout something.

"What is it?" he called back.

"Undertow!" she yelled.

Too late! The fish jerked left and a split second later Max hit the strange rippling current. The force of the water slammed Max and the bike sideways like a massive fist. The bike's engines groaned and squealed as he fought to right it, but he had no chance in the grip of the undertow. It threw him off the saddle, so he was only holding onto the handlebars with one fist, knuckles white. His other arm flailed in the water and it was suddenly hard to draw water into his gills. He felt like he was suffocating.

Boulders and sea shrubs streaked past on either side as the underwater torrent sucked him along, bouncing him off the seabed. Max caught flashes of the silver fish, also swept up in the undertow, but always just ahead. He saw Rivet too, barking madly and tumbling over and over in a tangle of useless leg propellers, waving paws and a flicking tail.

At least we're in this together! thought Max. But he couldn't get a breath, and his lungs felt crushed. It would be a terrible way to die. Had he been given the Merryn Touch, only to drown?

Black spots began to crowd in the edges of his vision.

There'd be no one to stop the Professor.

Sorry, Dad, he thought. *I've let you down…*

WIN AN EXCLUSIVE GOODY BAG

In every Sea Quest book the Sea Quest logo is hidden in one of the pictures. Find the logos in books 1 – 4, make a note of which pages they appear on and go online to enter the competition at

www.seaquestbooks.co.uk

Each month we will put all of the correct entries into a draw and select one winner to receive a special Sea Quest goody bag.

You can also send your entry on a postcard to:

Sea Quest Competition, Orchard Books, 338 Euston Road, London, NW1 3BH

Don't forget to include your name and address!

GOOD LUCK

Closing Date: June 1st 2013

SERIES 2:

THE CAVERN OF GHOSTS

OUT SEPTEMBER 2013

Dive into Sea Quest
and battle four new Robobeasts!

**SHREDDER THE SPIDER DROID
STINGER THE SEA PHANTOM
CRUSHER THE CREEPING TERROR
MANGLER THE DARK MENACE**

Watch out for the BRAND NEW
Special Bumper Edition

STENGOR THE CRAB MONSTER

OUT NOVEMBER 2013

DIVE INTO THIS UNDERWATER OFFER WITH

2 for 1 entry
at

Enjoy a journey of amazing discovery with this
special 2 for 1 deal!

Just cut out the voucher below and take it into your nearest
SEA LIFE centre or Sanctuary to take advantage
of this great offer.

Fancy diving beneath the sea without getting wet?

You'll come eyeball to eyeball with everything
from shrimps to sharks, and learn tons of great
stuff from SEA LIFE experts.
So go on, take the plunge and visit your
nearest SEA LIFE centre or Sanctuary soon!

Code: Sea Quest 13